THE HIPPOS' WEDDING

✦✦Lindsay Grater✦✦

LESTER

PUBLISHING

LIMITED

Canadian Cataloguing in Publication Data

Grater, Lindsay, 1952-

ISBN 1-89555-12-4

I. Title.

PS8563.R3H5 1991   jC813'.54   C91-094397-4
PZ10.3.G73Hi 1991

Book design by Nightlight Graphics

Lester Publishing Limited
56 The Esplanade
Toronto, Ontario
Canada M5E 1A7

91 92 93 94   5 4 3 2 1

Printed and bound in Hong Kong

For Toby and Benedict

"Listen to this, everyone," Mother Hippo called to her family. "Cousin Flo is getting married to that nice Hugo! The wedding is in just three days' time."

"We shall have to leave tomorrow morning," said Father. "Flo's village is far away on the other side of the jungle."

The Hippos hurried indoors to show the invitation to Granny. She had not been well recently and they were sure that Flo's news would cheer her up.

During lunch Mother made a list of supplies needed for the journey. Then Father headed a piece of paper "Wedding Present Shopping List." Everybody thought hard for several minutes.

Granny suggested a lacy tablecloth. She said sadly that the long trip to the wedding would be too tiring for her, but her gift would be light enough for the others to carry.

Rosie, who loved to eat, thought a cookbook would be in good taste.

Rollo, who loved to draw and paint, decided that a picture would be an attractive gift.

Mother and Father, who were warmhearted and generous, chose a huge feather-filled quilt. Starry nights in the jungle could be chilly.

Once the serious shopping was completed that afternoon, the Hippos treated themselves to some little presents.

Granny bought four rolls of film so the family could take loads of wedding pictures for her.

Rollo could not resist some fancy rainbow suspenders and Rosie picked some ribbons the exact clover pink of her best dress.

Father found a wonderful tie to match the suit he would wear to the wedding.

Mother's treat was not quite so little, but she said she could not possibly go to a wedding without a new hat.

That evening, the bags were packed and everyone went to bed early.

1001 THINGS TO DO WITH TROPICAL FRUIT

At sunrise, Mother and Father Hippo, Rollo and Rosie kissed Granny good bye and started their journey.

"Keep your eyes and your ears open," warned Granny. "The jungle is full of beauty and full of surprises, some of them nice — some of them nasty."

The jungle was beautiful. Everything in it seemed larger than life. There were flowers the size of buckets and butterflies as big as books. The Hippos marvelled at the sight and smell of giant jungle roses. But roses have thorns and huge roses have huge thorns. One hooked a looping thread of the delicate tablecloth in Father Hippo's backpack and the whole thing unraveled.

Suddenly Father Hippo realized that his bag was feeling lighter. He gave it a little squeeze. It was horribly empty. Behind him, the jungle was tied in thread, like a spider's web.

The travelers froze. How were they going to explain this to Granny? The tablecloth had been her gift to the bride and groom.

"Never mind," said Mother. "We still have the other three gifts."

The Hippos were worn out by the long walk and the disappointment about the tablecloth. They nibbled halfheartedly at their supper and made camp for the night.

"We must make sure that nothing happens to the other presents," said Mother.

She wrapped the cookbook, the painting and the quilt in strong leaves to protect them from the damp night air. Then she tucked them carefully under a bush.

The four exhausted Hippos curled up and slept deeply.

During the night something ate holes in the cookbook.

Rosie burst into tears when she discovered the damage to her gift. Father made her a bracing cup of mint tea by boiling some water over the burning remains of the book.

Rosie sipped and sobbed until it was time to pack up and move on.

Rosie sulked about her cookbook as she walked along. She thought a sweet little treat might cheer her up so she bent down to grab a bunch of fat berries. Beneath the berry bush was a snake which sprang up to grab fat little Rosie. She squealed, staggered and rolled down the riverbank. The painting which Rollo had chosen so carefully flew from her backpack and plopped into the water.

Rosie was rescued but the painting was ruined. Rollo was very upset.

"At least our last present is safe," said Mother. "And so is your sister."

Now that the quilt was the only present left, it seemed doubly precious. Rollo held it tightly for his mother while he rode on her back.

The Hippos trudged along by the river for many hours. Their minds dwelt on the three disasters of the trip.

In the water lurked the cause of disaster number four.

Rollo, bobbing above the reeds, was a temptation that no hungry crocodile could resist. The massive jaws lunged and snapped and ripped a chunk out of . . . the quilt.

The crocodile's eyes, ears, nostrils and mouth were stuffed with feathers. He snuffled and groped his way back to the river.

"That's that, then," wailed Mother as she clutched Rollo. "We can't possibly go to the wedding with no presents. We shall have to go home!"

"Remember, it's us that Hugo and Flo want to see," said Father, "not fancy presents. Let's stop now for the night. Things will look better in the morning."

There were sad thoughts in the jungle that night. Sad thoughts about presents as the Hippos drifted off to sleep.

Mother remembered going to a birthday party when she was little. She had carried a beautifully wrapped gift to her best friend's house — only to find that she had come on the wrong day . . .

Father thought of his own sixth birthday. For some reason his grandmother had forgotten to send him a present. She gave him a lovely one a week later but it just hadn't been the same . . .

Rosie was thinking about all the New Baby presents that had been given to Rollo when he was born. But nobody had brought her anything . . .

And Rollo remembered how furious he had been as a baby when his big sister had walked off with all his New Baby presents and left him stranded in his crib . . .

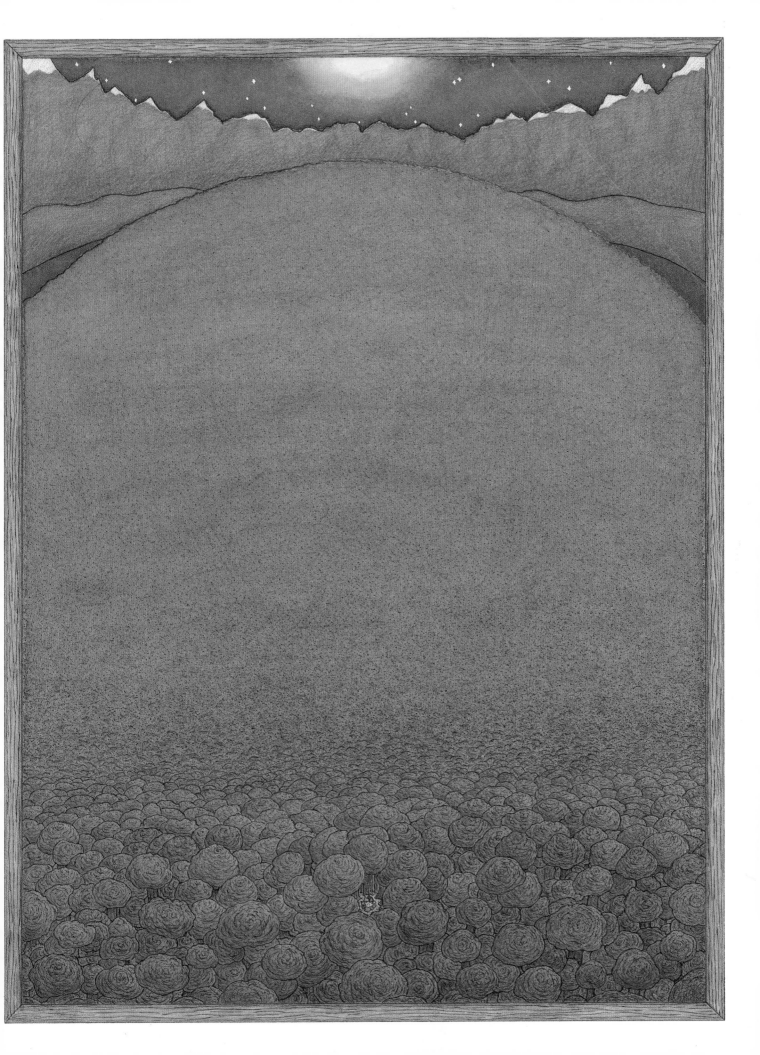

Dawn in the jungle was glorious. It filled the waking Hippos with hope.

"This afternoon," announced Mother, "we shall be at Flo and Hugo's wedding. And this morning," she added firmly, "we are going to replace all those lost presents!"

Father, Rosie and Rollo nodded in agreement, although they had no idea how this would be achieved.

"We shall have to improvise," added Mother, seeing the doubt in their faces.

They marched along the path, searching for inspiration.

Soon they came to a sparkling waterfall. It was fringed with mosses and ferns.

"Those lacy ferns remind me of Granny's tablecloth," sighed Father. "In fact," he continued thoughtfully, "they would make a very pretty table decoration for a special occasion . . . like a WEDDING!"

"If only we could climb those slippery rocks to reach them," added Mother wistfully.

The problem was solved by some kind ants. They nipped off huge bunches of ferns and carried them down to the Hippos.

Further on, wild chattering attracted the Hippos' attention. Dozens of excited monkeys were having a feast in a mango tree.

"I have a brilliant idea!" shouted Mother. "Instead of fruit recipes in a cookbook, let's take real fruit to the wedding!"

All four Hippos called up to the highest branches.

"Please, please throw us some juicy mangoes! We need them for a wedding present!"

The playful monkeys had a mango-dropping contest and soon the ground was thick with fruit.

The edge of the jungle was not far away now. Flowers filled the sunny patches between the thinning trees.

"These flowers are as pretty as a picture," remarked Mother.

"Better than a picture!" yelled Rosie as she started to pick an enormous bouquet for Flo and Hugo.

"Now all we have to replace is the quilt," said Father, "but we must be quick. The wedding starts soon."

Little Rollo looked up at a pair of parrots on a branch. "Could you birds help us, please?" he asked.

"We can't give you a feather quilt," squawked one parrot, "but we can lend you a feathered choir."

The pair screeched a shrill message across the treetops. Soon they were joined by a crowd of brilliantly colored birds, all willing to sing at the wedding.

The problem of the presents was solved. Now it was time to get ready for the wedding. Out came the new suspenders and tie, the bows and the hat. In their party clothes the Hippos left the last trees of the jungle with light steps.

As they entered the village, Flo ran to greet them. She wore a beautiful white wedding dress. Amid many hugs and kisses the Hippos spilled out the tale of their dreadful journey. But they found that the bad memories had already begun to fade.

"Well," said Flo, "your company is the best present ever. And how clever of you to bring gifts which we can use right now. Let's spread them out on the tables for all the guests to enjoy."

That evening there was a sumptuous wedding feast. The flowers and ferns made the tables beautiful. The guests munched on the sweet mangoes and thrilled to the dazzling bird choir.

"Your lovely gifts won't last forever," said Flo. "The fruit will be eaten, the ferns and flowers will fade and the birds will fly away. But they *will* last forever in our memories — and in our wedding photographs."

"Now," said Hugo as he cut the wedding cake, "we certainly don't want this to last forever! Let's start eating it!"

And everyone laughed roundly beneath the starlit tropical sky.